The Wizard of Oz

retold by Mary Carey

illustrated by Don Turner/Jason Studios

Based on the best-loved children's classic THE
WONDERFUL WIZARD OF OZ by L. Frank Baum

gb GOLDEN PRESS

Western Publishing Company, Inc.
Racine, Wisconsin

D1106736

Second Printing, 1976

© 1975 by Western Publishing Company, Inc.
All rights reserved. Produced in U.S.A.

GOLDEN, A LITTLE GOLDEN BOOK®, and GOLDEN PRESS®
are trademarks of Western Publishing Company, Inc. No part
of this book may be reproduced or copied in any form without
written permission from the publisher.

Once there was a little girl named Dorothy, who lived on a farm in Kansas. She lived with her Uncle Henry and her Auntie Em and her little dog, Toto.

Nothing very exciting ever happened on that farm —until the day of the big wind. It was a wind called a tornado, and it came roaring across the fields, scattering haystacks and chicken coops and tree branches every which way.

Then it roared and twisted around the farmhouse, and it picked up the house, Dorothy, Toto, and all!

The wind carried the house high, high into the air. It carried the house far, far from Kansas. Then it set the house down with a soft *whump*.

It set the house down in a place where there were green hills and sparkling blue streams and, of all things, crowds of strange little people.

"Welcome to Munchkin Land," said one little man to Dorothy.

"Thank you," said Dorothy politely. "It's very pretty here, but how can I get home to Kansas? My Auntie Em and Uncle Henry will be worried about Toto and me."

The little man had never heard of Kansas. None of the little people had ever heard of Kansas.

"My dear," said a nice old lady, "you must go to the Emerald City and ask Oz, the Great Wizard, how to get to Kansas. Oz is very wise and wonderful, and he will know about Kansas, if anyone does."

"Follow the yellow brick road, and you can't go wrong," said a little gentleman. "It will take you right to the Emerald City."

So Dorothy and Toto set off down the yellow brick road. Before long, they came to a cornfield, and there was a Scarecrow, stuck up on a pole.

He was a most unusual Scarecrow. He could nod and wink and even talk. When he learned that Dorothy and Toto were going to see the wizard, he decided that he would go, too. "Perhaps the mighty wizard could give me some brains," he said.

Dorothy agreed that even a Scarecrow would be better off with a brain or two, so she helped him down off his pole and over the fence.

After a bit, Dorothy and Toto and the Scarecrow saw, beside the road, a man who was made entirely of tin. He stood holding an ax, but he didn't speak and he didn't stir.

"Why, he's all rusted," said Dorothy. She ran to a nearby cottage, where she found an oilcan. Then she oiled the Tin Woodman's joints very carefully.

The Tin Woodman was ever so grateful that he could move once more. And when he heard that Dorothy and the Scarecrow were going to see the Great Wizard, he asked if he might come, too.

"Perhaps Oz would give me a heart," he said. "It's most difficult to be without a heart. I want to love people, but one needs a heart for that."

"I suppose one does," said Dorothy. "All right, come along with us."

"And let's take the oilcan," said the Scarecrow. "We don't want you to rust again."

So off they all went, down the yellow brick road —Dorothy and Toto, the Scarecrow, the Tin Woodman, and, of course, the oilcan.

Suddenly there was a terrible roar, and a huge lion sprang onto the road. He opened his enormous mouth and showed his sharp teeth. It seemed he wanted to gobble Toto up.

"Don't you dare!" cried Dorothy, rushing at the lion and slapping him on the nose.

The lion stopped roaring and began to cry.

"Why, you're just a big coward," said Dorothy.

"I know," sobbed the lion. "I can't help it. I was born this way."

Dorothy and her friends felt so sorry for the wretched, weeping lion that they invited him to come with them. "Perhaps the mighty Oz will give you some courage," said Dorothy.

The Cowardly Lion wanted courage more than he
wanted anything, so he was happy to journey to the
Emerald City of Oz.

As night was coming on, the travelers saw a great
castle near the road.

"Oh, dear!" The Cowardly Lion shivered. "Oh,
my! The Wicked Witch of the West lives there. Let's
hide! Quickly!"

Too late! The Wicked Witch had already seen them. "Travelers on the road!" she screeched, and she called her winged monkeys.

"The tin man and the scarecrow are of no use," she told the monkeys. "Destroy them, but bring the little girl and the dog and the lion to me!"

The winged monkeys swooped down upon Dorothy and her friends. They hurled the Tin Woodman from a cliff, and he lay below, bent and battered.

They tore the straw from the Scarecrow and tossed his clothes into a tree, so there was nothing left of him but that bundle of old clothes.

But Dorothy, Toto, and the Cowardly Lion were carried to the Wicked Witch.

"You'll scrub my floors and wash my dishes," said
the witch to Dorothy. "As for your lion, he'll pull my
chariot!"

"I will not!" said the Cowardly Lion, and he said
it in a very brave way.

"You will, or I'll put you in a cage!" said the
Wicked Witch.

"You cruel thing!" cried Dorothy, and though she was really a gentle girl, she picked up a bucket of water and threw it over the witch.

"Oh, oh, oh!" screamed the witch. "Now look what you've done! You've ruined me!"

And there, right before Dorothy's eyes, the Wicked Witch of the West melted away like snow under the summer sun.

Dorothy and Toto and the Cowardly Lion fled from that horrid castle.

They quickly found the Tin Woodman. They hammered the dents out of his arms and legs so that he was almost as good as new.

They found the Scarecrow's empty clothes and
stuffed them with fresh straw. There was the Scarecrow again, whole and as happy as ever.

Then they hurried on until they reached the green,
gleaming, sparkling Emerald City of Oz.

When the Great Wizard, Oz, learned that the travelers at his gates had melted the Wicked Witch of the West, he consented to see them.

He was not exactly what Dorothy had expected. He was a timid little man, who hid behind his emerald throne when they first came in. However, he was also a wise little man.

"You want brains, do you?" he said to the Scarecrow. He took the straw out of the Scarecrow's head and put a big heap of pins and needles in its place.

"Now you're bristling with good, sharp brains," said he. "Use them, and you'll be as clever as can be."

"The Scarecrow is clever already," whispered Dorothy.

"I suspected as much," said the wizard.

Then into the Tin Woodman's chest, the wizard put a pretty little heart made of red satin.

"The Tin Woodman has been tenderhearted all along," said Dorothy.

"I imagined so," replied the wizard.

The wizard then gave the Cowardly Lion a magic potion, and the lion gulped down every drop. When he finished, he roared louder than any three lions. "I feel so brave!" he cried.

"You were already brave," the wizard told him. "Courage means doing what's right, even if you feel afraid while you're doing it."

"Now, what about Kansas?" asked Dorothy.

The Great Wizard smiled and took a pair of pretty silver slippers out of his pocket. "These are truly magic," he said. "Put them on, and they'll take you wherever you want to go."

So Dorothy put on the slippers, said good-bye to her friends, picked up Toto, and thought, "Kansas!"

In a twinkling, the Emerald City was gone. Back she was in Kansas. Auntie Em was hugging her. Uncle Henry was wiping his eyes and laughing, and Toto was barking.

She was home again! And of all the wonderful places she had been, home was the best place to be!

10 DAY FREE TRIAL

THE FOUR WONDERFUL WORLDS OF
WALT DISNEY

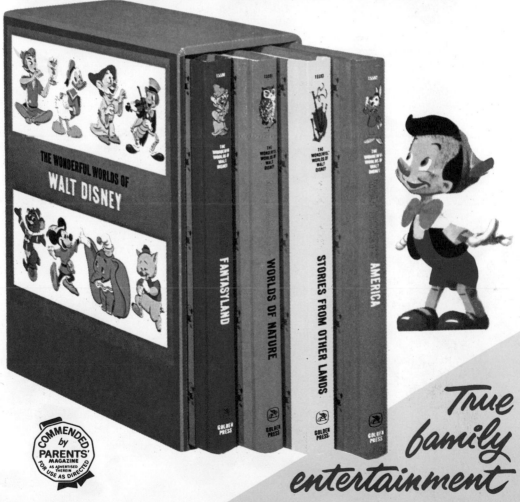

THE WONDERFUL WORLDS OF
WALT DISNEY

FANTASYLAND

WORLDS OF NATURE

STORIES FROM OTHER LANDS

AMERICA

COMMENDED by PARENTS' MAGAZINE AS ADVERTISED THEREIN FOR USE AS DIRECTED

GOLDEN PRESS

True family entertainment

BACK BY POPULAR DEMAND!
OVER 2 MILLION DELIGHTED CUSTOMERS

* 4 beautiful volumes
* 64 magical stories
* Over 1,000 pages
* FREE Disney Poster

AT LAST, into your home comes the magic of the greatest story teller of our time—64 of Walt Disney's greatest film stories are assembled in permanent book form—for the delight of your entire family! And you can examine them in your own home for ten days free. This enchanting collection of the young in heart comes in four sumptuous, giant-sized volumes...7½" x 10½"... over 1,000 pages in full color...in a handsome slipcase. In addition, you will also receive FREE a large Disney poster just for examining this set of books.

© Walt Disney Productions

FANTASYLAND. You'll go adventuring with Cinderella, the Ugly Duckling, Snow White, the Sleeping Beauty, Peter and the Wolf, and ten other favorite Disney characters—all brought to life in words and glowing color!

WORLDS OF NATURE. Real worlds more amazing than any fairy tale: *The Living Desert, Secrets of Life, The African Lion, The Vanishing Prairie*—plus two beloved stories, *Perri* and *Bambi*. Color photographs from the original Disney films are reproduced on quality paper.

AMERICA. *The Uncle Remus* stories . . . tales such as *Johnny Appleseed* and *Davy Crockett*, stories such as *The Shaggy Dog* and *The Flying Car* . . . excursions with Pollyanna and Old Yeller . . . stories the whole family will enjoy.

STORIES FROM OTHER LANDS. Fourteen of the most delightful Walt Disney creations you've thrilled to on the screen—*Stories from Other Lands, Swiss Family Robinson, Sword in the Stone, Robin Hood, Alice in Wonderland, 101 Dalmatians,* and eight more.

DETACH AND MAIL THIS POSTPAID CARD TODAY!

Golden Press, Dept. T3
175 Community Drive
Lake Success Park, Great Neck, N.Y. 11025

Please send me **THE FOUR WONDERFUL WORLDS OF WALT DISNEY** for free 10-day examination. I understand that I can return the four volumes to you without obligation within 10 days, if I am not delighted with them. *The cost of credit is included in the price quoted for the goods and services.* If I decide to keep them you will bill me at the low price of just $4.99 a month for five months (a total of only $24.95). A small charge will be added to your first invoice for postage, handling and local sales tax. THERE ARE NO FINANCE CHARGES. I understand that the FREE POSTER is mine to keep even if I return the books.

Name_____

Address_____

City_____State_____Zip_____

Parent's Signature_____

AVAILABLE BY MAIL ORDER ONLY.

THE FOUR WONDERFUL WORLDS OF
WALT DISNEY

The perfect gift for any occasion—
enjoyment for the entire family.

"Please send me three more sets. I've found them so lovely, I'm anxious to give them to others."
—Mrs. J. A., Franklin Square, N.Y.

"These books are truly a beautiful creation of art and literature. Thank you profoundly!"
—P. B. M., Cincinnati, Ohio

SEND NO MONEY.
JUST MAIL THE COUPON TODAY!

Golden Press

A Division of Western Publishing Co., Inc.
175 Community Drive, Lake Success Park, Great Neck, N.Y. 11025

FIRST CLASS
PERMIT NO. 1064
GREAT NECK, N.Y.

BUSINESS REPLY MAIL
NO POSTAGE STAMP NECESSARY IF MAILED IN THE UNITED STATES

POSTAGE WILL BE PAID BY

GOLDEN PRESS
A Division of Western Publishing Co., Inc.
175 COMMUNITY DRIVE
LAKE SUCCESS PARK,
GREAT NECK, N.Y. 11025

Dept. T3